Minnie's World

Written by Katie Kobble

It's fun to be Minnie.
She has poise. She has style.
What a sweet dress!
And look at that smile!

Her life is so dreamy.
Her world is a whirl
of all the fun things
that delight any girl.

Shopping for dresses
and cute shoes and bows.

What girl wouldn't squeal over fancy new clothes?

Planning a picnic
with good things to eat.

Cooking and prepping!

Oh, my! What a treat!

It's neat being Minnie.
Her world is so sunny—
with good food and friends
who are happy and funny.

It's great to be lazy
with Daisy all day,

while the boys pitch a tent . . .

And then they all play!

When the work is all done
and the fun is unfurled,
it's always a play day
in cute Minnie's world!

In fall, all her friends have a ball at her house.

Parties! Fiestas!
Hooray, Minnie Mouse!

In winter, it's wonderful.
Step, glide, and twirl!

Mickey goes sledding with his favorite girl.

In spring, Minnie's garden is one big bouquet.

In summer, her yard
is the best place to be.

With splatters and sprinklers,
it's one splashing spree!

Wheeee!
It's great to be Minnie!
She's spunky and fun!

Wherever she goes, she charms everyone.

With her bow set just right,
and her eyelashes curled,
sweet Minnie sits pretty
in her perfect world.